For Pam and Helen,
*a bloke couldn't ask for
two better sisters...
and believe me, I tried.*
A.S.

For Anne, Chris, Helena,
Jo and Kim.
H.A.

First published in 2004
by Meadowside Children's Books,
185 Fleet Street, London, EC4A 2HS

Text © Alec Sillifant 2004
Illustration © Heather Allen 2004

The rights of Alec Sillifant to be identified
as the author and Heather Allen to be
identified as the illustrator of this work
have been asserted by them in
accordance with the Copyright.
Designs and Patents Act, 1988

A CIP catalogue record for this book
is available from the British Library

Printed in U.A.E

10 9 8 7 6 5 4 3 2 1

Little Green Monsters

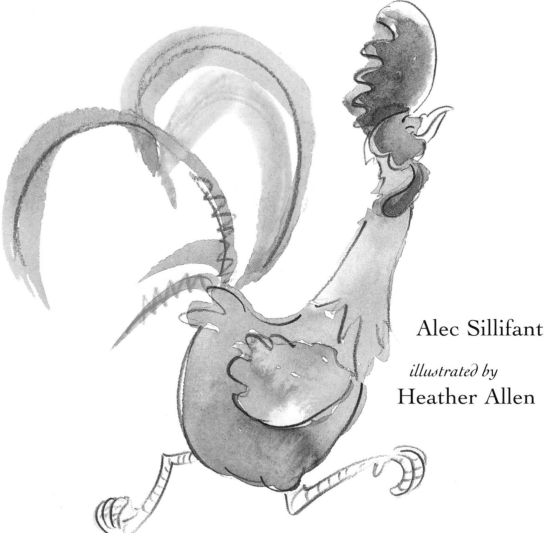

Alec Sillifant

illustrated by
Heather Allen

meadowside
CHILDREN'S BOOKS

It was Errol's first day as rooster of Seed Lane Chicken Farm and he was very nervous.

In fact, he was so nervous he hadn't slept a wink the night before.

"Cock-a-

doodle-do!"

Errol wanted to prove he was the best rooster for the job, so as soon as the sun came up he made sure he was ready to cry 'Cock-a-doodle-do' at the top of his voice.

After waking all
the chickens,
Errol decided to
explore, and the
chicken shed seemed
the best place to start.

As he wandered
about, Errol noticed
little piles of straw in
the boxes the
chickens slept in,
each of which
contained a funny
shaped object.

Suddenly a chicken from behind said. "They're eggs."

Errol hadn't known what they were but he didn't want to look foolish on his first day.

"I knew that," he lied, and with a smile he walked off to explore some more of the farm.

Next Errol walked to the farmhouse and hopped onto a window ledge to take a look inside and there he could see the farmer's television.

"How strange," thought the rooster. "There are some more of those egg things."

Errol watched in amazement as the eggs on the television twitched...

and wobbled...

and bounced...

and bobbled...

until...

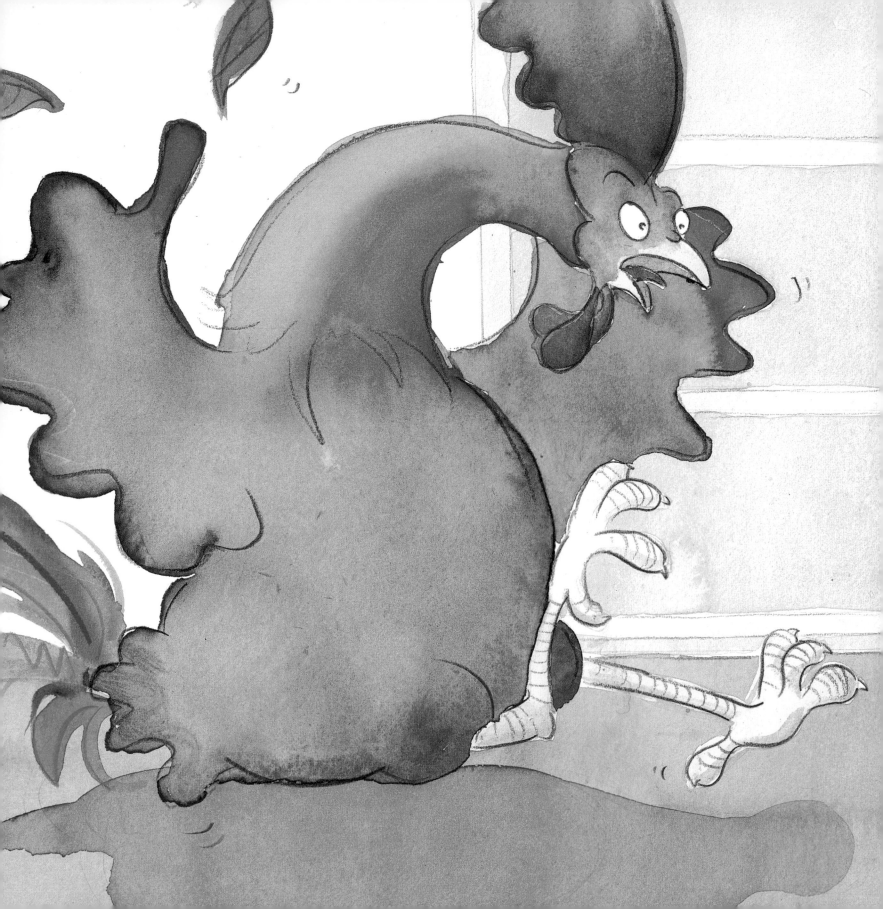

CRrRAAACK!!!

One of the eggs
burst open!

Errol fell off
the window
ledge in fright
at what he
had seen
and ran at
full speed,
wings
flapping
wildly,
back to the
shed shouting,
**"Little Green
Monsters!!"**

Inside the shed Errol began to gather all the eggs together.

"What are you doing?" said one of the chickens.

"I've got to save the farm from little green monsters!"

"Little green monsters?!" shrieked a chicken.

"No time to explain," said Errol. "Just help me to get rid of these eggs!"

"The monsters will get out!" screamed Errol struggling to stand up. "I saw it on the television… the monsters will get out!"

"Shhhhh!" hissed one of the chickens. "Listen!"

"They're hatching," smiled one of the chickens.

"We've got to get out of here," sobbed Errol. "We've got to run away."

"Quiet!" said another chicken. "Watch what happens."

Errol looked at the eggs and saw they were twitching... wobbling... bouncing... and bobbling...

He closed his eyes...

If he was going to be eaten by little green monsters he didn't want to see it happen.

Errol kept his eyes shut until a chicken tapped him on the head and said, "You can open your eyes now."

Errol slowly opened one eye, and then the other. "Where are the little green monsters?" he said.

The chickens laughed. "There never were any little green monsters in the eggs, just these."

Errol was so relieved at what he saw that he laughed too as the tiny, chirping, yellow chicks jumped around at his feet.

One day, many, many months later, Errol found an egg, half buried in the mud by the river.

Errol decided it was his duty, as a good rooster, to take it back to the chicken shed so that it could hatch safely with all the other eggs.

Luckily for Errol, the
crocodile who had left it
there didn't see him take it.

Then again, perhaps it
would have been
better if she
had…